Dear Parent:

Congratulations! Your child is taking the first steps on an exciting journey. The destination? Independent reading!

STEP INTO READING® will help your child get there. The program offers five steps to reading success. Each step includes fun stories and colorful art. There are also Step into Reading Sticker Books, Step into Reading Math Readers, Step into Reading Write-In Readers, Step into Reading Phonics Readers, and Step into Reading Phonics First Steps! Boxed Sets—a complete literacy program with something for every child.

Learning to Read, Step by Step!

Ready to Read Preschool–Kindergarten
• big type and easy words • rhyme and rhythm • picture clues
For children who know the alphabet and are eager to begin reading.

Reading with Help Preschool–Grade 1
• basic vocabulary • short sentences • simple stories
For children who recognize familiar words and sound out new words with help.

Reading on Your Own Grades 1–3
• engaging characters • easy-to-follow plots • popular topics
For children who are ready to read on their own.

Reading Paragraphs Grades 2–3
• challenging vocabulary • short paragraphs • exciting stories
For newly independent readers who read simple sentences with confidence.

Ready for Chapters Grades 2–4
• chapters • longer paragraphs • full-color art
For children who want to take the plunge into chapter books but still like colorful pictures.

STEP INTO READING® is designed to give every child a successful reading experience. The grade levels are only guides. Children can progress through the steps at their own speed, developing confidence in their reading, no matter what their grade.

Remember, a lifetime love of reading starts with a single step!

For Hailey and Lilly—M.L.

Visit us on the Web!
www.stepintoreading.com
www.randomhouse.com/kids

Educators and librarians, for a variety of teaching tools, visit us at
www.randomhouse.com/teachers

Library of Congress Cataloging-in-Publication Data
Lagonegro, Melissa.
Kiss the frog / by Melissa Lagonegro.
p. cm. — (Step into reading. Step 2 book)
ISBN 978-0-7364-2614-5 (trade) — ISBN 978-0-7364-8073-4 (lib. bdg.)
I. Kiss the frog (Motion picture). II. Title. PZ7.L14317Kis 2009 [E]—dc22 2008054177

Printed in the United States of America   27 26 25 24 23 22 21 20 19 18

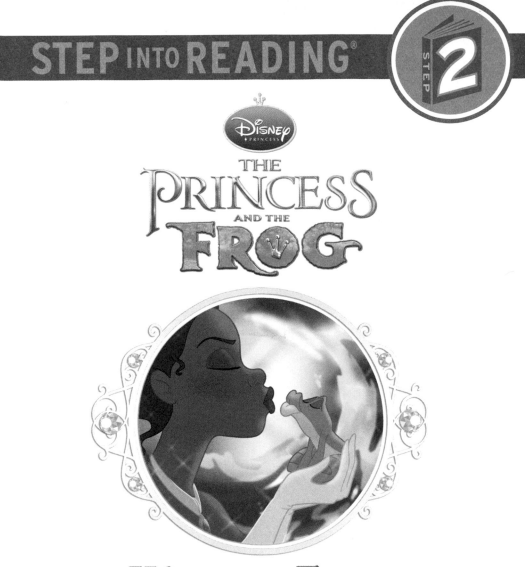

DISNEY PRINCESS

THE PRINCESS AND THE FROG

Kiss the Frog

By Melissa Lagonegro

Illustrated by Elizabeth Tate, Caroline LaVelle Egan,

Studio IBOIX, Michael Inman, and the Disney Storybook Artists

Random House 🏠 New York

Tiana works hard.
She has no time
for fun.

She has a dream.
She wants to own
a restaurant.

Prince Naveen
likes to have fun.

He loves music.

He visits New Orleans.

Facilier is a bad man.

He plans to trick

Naveen.

Facilier uses bad magic.

He turns Prince Naveen

into a frog!

Tiana goes
to a costume party.
She wishes on a star.
She wishes
for her restaurant.
Naveen sees her.

Tiana meets Naveen.
She looks like a princess.
Naveen thinks her kiss
will make him human.
He wants to kiss Tiana.

Tiana kisses Naveen.
But she is not
a real princess.

The kiss does not work!

Naveen is still a frog.

Tiana turns

into a frog,

too!

Tiana and Naveen
get lost.
They do not like
being frogs.
They do not like
each other.

They meet
Louis the alligator.
Naveen has fun!
Tiana does not.

The frogs try
to catch a bug.
They get stuck together.

Ray is a firefly.

He helps the frogs.

They all become friends.

Tiana shows Naveen
how to cook.

They like
each other now.

Tiana and Naveen
find Mama Odie.

She makes good magic.

She can help them.

Mama Odie

shows Naveen

a princess.

He must kiss her.
Then he and Tiana will
become human again!

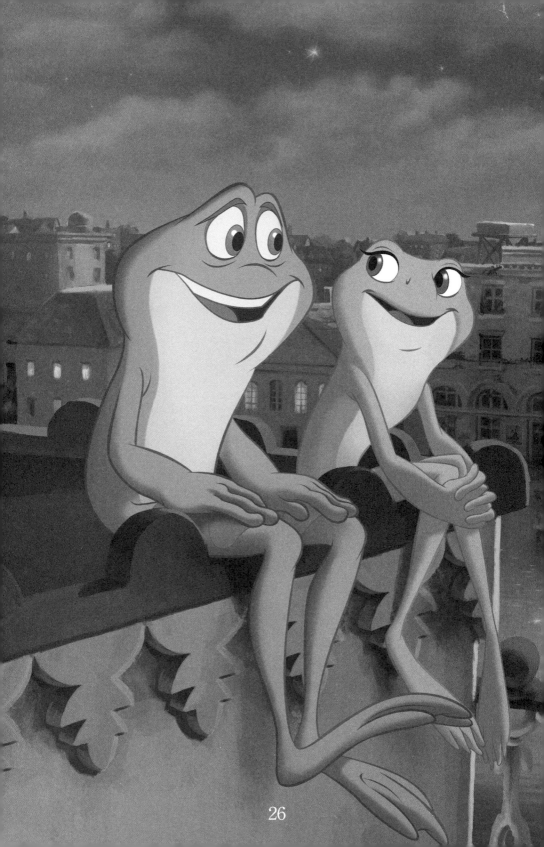

Tiana and Naveen
are happy!
They are in love.

Naveen kisses a princess.

But it is too late.

The spell does not break!

Naveen is still a frog.

Tiana is still a frog.

Tiana and Prince Naveen
go back to Mama Odie.
They get married.

Now Tiana is
a <u>real</u> princess.
They kiss. <u>POOF!</u>
They become human again!

Tiana's dream comes true.

She gets her restaurant.

She has love.

She has everything

she needs!